W9-BGL-952

This Book Belongs to:

Martha -
We are so thankful
for you & how special
you make Thanksgiving
each year!

Love,
Jim & Sharon
Josh & Leigha
2004

Thanksgiving
What Makes It Special?

Harold Myra

ILLUSTRATED BY JANE KURISU

www.tommynelson.com

A Division of Thomas Nelson, Inc.
www.ThomasNelson.com

For Lindsey, Josh, and Rick

Copyright © 2002 by Harold Myra

Illustrations copyright © 2002 by Jane Kurisu

All rights reserved. No portion of this book may be
reproduced in any form without written permission from the publisher,
with the exception of brief excerpts in reviews.

Published in Nashville, Tennessee, by Tommy Nelson®, a division of Thomas Nelson, Inc.

Library of Congress Cataloging-in-Publication Data

Myra, Harold Lawrence, 1939–
    Thanksgiving: what makes it special? / Harold Myra ; illustrated by Jane Kurisu.
        p. cm.
    Summary: As they prepare to celebrate Thanksgiving Day, Todd and his family discuss
the meaning of the holiday and its relationship to their Christian beliefs.
    ISBN 1-4003-0006-1
    [1. Thanksgiving Day—Fiction. 2. Christian life—Fiction.] I. Kurisu, Jane, 1952– ill.
II. Title.
PZ7.M9954 The 2002
[E]—dc21

Printed in Singapore
02 03 04 05 06 TWP 5 4 3 2 1

A Note to Parents

We all recognize Thanksgiving as a national
holiday with rich, deep meaning. Yet we are
also tempted to make it just another four-day
weekend.

Most of us today enjoy an abundance of
blessings. It's more vital than ever that we
model for our children deep gratitude to God
and a sharing of our bounty. My hope is that
this book will help parents and children truly
celebrate this biblical and historic day.

—Harold Myra

Happy Turkey Day!" sang the radio announcer.

"Grrrrreat weather for football!"

"Turkey Day?" said Greg. "What's that mean?"

Dad scrunched his eyebrows. "She means Thanksgiving," said Dad. "Sometimes people call it 'Turkey Day.'"

Greg's older brother grinned. "Kids at school call it Pig-Out Day," he said.

"That's too bad, Todd," said Mom. "Thanksgiving isn't really Turkey Day or Pig-Out Day!" She checked the pies in the oven while Michelle dropped cranberries into a grinder.

"I learned about it in school," said Michelle. "It started when the Pilgrims thanked God."

"Oh, yeah!" said Todd. "And the Pilgrims wore those funny clothes."

"They just dressed differently from us," said Michelle. "They would probably think we wear funny clothes!"

"Not me!" said Todd and tugged on his jeans.

Michelle tossed a cranberry at him.

"You know, half the Pilgrims died that first winter," Michelle said. "But the Native Americans helped them. They shared their seeds and taught the Pilgrims how to plant crops that grew in America. So the next year, the Pilgrims had a good harvest. They had enough to eat."

"Yeah," said Todd. "Plus they fished and hunted. They found deer and ducks!"

Michelle nodded. "They even had a feast. They invited their Native American neighbors, and ninety people came to eat with the Pilgrims."

"It was sort of a potluck dinner," Dad said. "The Native Americans brought five deer. And everyone feasted together for three whole days."

"How cool is that?" Mom added. "They also served wild turkey. Plus they had fish, oysters, and tons of veggies. It takes a lot of work to feed 140 people!"

"They didn't even have ovens," said Dad. "They cooked Thanksgiving dinner over an open fire."

"So, Dad," said Todd, "what's so bad about calling it 'Turkey Day'?"

"Well, son, it's because Thanksgiving isn't just about turkey," said Dad. "It's about being thankful. And we show we're thankful when we praise God. The Pilgrims knew this.

"They shared their bounty with one another. They were thankful that God enabled them to provide. And provide they did— enough for themselves *and* their neighbors."

"I get it now," said Todd.

"Me too," said Michelle. "It's just what the Bible says, 'Give thanks! Make a joyful noise to the Lord!'"

"I can make noise!" said Greg. He *rat-tat-tatted* a rhythm on his drum.

Next, Michelle and Greg decorated the windows. They waited for their cousins to arrive.

"Good job," said Dad. "Too bad we don't have a Moses decal. He's part of Thanksgiving too."

"Moses?" said Michelle. "When did he visit America?"

Dad laughed. "Long before our Pilgrims were around, Moses commanded a full week of Thanksgiving."

"Oh," said Michelle. "Like all through the Bible, there are stories where people give thanks to God."

"Exactly!" said Dad.

"But sometimes," said Todd, "people just think about turkey or football. When they think of Thanksgiving, they think of food."

"That's true," said Dad. "We need to keep the 'thanks' in Thanksgiving. Even Jesus knew people who weren't thankful. Remember the story of the ten lepers?"

"Jesus healed them, didn't He?" asked Todd.

"He sure did," said Dad. "But only one man came back. He kneeled at Jesus' feet. He was full of gratitude.

"You see, Thanksgiving means thanking God for everything—for the breath in our lungs, for our loved ones. We need to be thankful for all He provides."

"I'm thankful," said Todd as he eyed the cooling pies.

"Good for you," said Mom. "Jesus was thankful too. He constantly thanked His heavenly Father."

"Thank You, Jesus," said Greg.

"Thank you, Greg," said Mom.

Dad crunched on a carrot. "Giving thanks is even better for you than eating vegetables."

Michelle cocked her head. "What?"

"Anything's better than vegetables!" Todd whispered.

"Really," said Dad. "A scientific study proved that being thankful makes you feel healthy. So when you're thankful, your body almost purrs like a happy kitten."

"So at dinner," said Mom, "let's count our blessings before we load up our plates."

"I'm thankful for hot pecan rolls," said Todd. "What are you thankful for?"

"Legos!" shouted Greg.

Dad pointed. "I'm thankful for sunshine and red maple leaves."

Michelle said, "I'm thankful for friends and family. And God."

Dad winked. "I see you've been listening at Sunday school."

"God loved us so much He sent us Jesus. Now that's really a reason to be thankful!"

"And Jesus wants us to share everything," Mom said.

"I share my Legos!" said Greg.

"Perfect!" said Mom.

"And we share our family with foster kids," Michelle added.

"We sure do," said Mom. "It feels good to make others
happy. We're thankful we can share what we have."

"Thanksgiving does mean sharing," said Dad. "The Native Americans shared seeds with the Pilgrims, and later they all shared a feast together. They were thankful to have each other.

"Just like we're thankful for all of you. Let's show God how grateful we are by keeping the 'thanks' in Thanksgiving!"